ONE DAY, LONG AGO

One Day, Long Ago

More stories from a Shona Childhood

Charles Mungoshi

Illustrated by Luke Toronga

First published in 1991
by Baobab Books
a division of Academic Books (Pvt.) Ltd
P.O. Box 567, Harare, Zimbabwe

© Charles Mungoshi

Illustrations: Luke Toronga
Typeset by Academic Books
Printed by
National Printing and Packaging, Harare

ISBN 0-908311-30-3

Publication of this book has been made
possible by the generous support of the
Canadian Organization for Development
through Education (CODE).

Contents

Hare's Medicine Bag 7

The Prince and the Leper 27

The Blind Man and the Lion 41

The Lazy Young Man and his Dog 53

FRONTISPIECE: *There was a thick cloud of dust as the young man and his dog rolled in front of the Chief and his daughter. (See page 59).*

Hare's Medicine Bag

Hare and Baboon were neighbours. They were also great friends. Hare had a son, Nhowa, whom he loved very much. Baboon had no children.

One day, Baboon said to Hare, 'I want to visit my relatives. It is a long journey and I would like to have someone to talk to on the way. Would you please let your son come with me?'

'Very well,' agreed Hare.

'I shall provide the food we will need for the journey, so do not trouble your wife to prepare any for us,' Baboon explained.

'Very well,' said Hare.

The following morning Baboon and Nhowa started out very early on their journey. Baboon, however, was not carrying any provisions as he had promised to do. Nhowa was young and he was too excited to notice that Baboon was not carrying any food for their journey.

On and on they travelled. The sun rose and on they went. The sun climbed high in the sky and still they travelled on.

'Uncle Baboon,' Nhowa said, 'I am thirsty.'

'Wait till we get to the Makudo River,' replied Baboon. 'It isn't very far from here.'

When they reached the river, Nhowa had stooped down for a good long drink, when Baboon shouted, 'Hold it!'

Surprised, Nhowa looked at Baboon and asked, 'Why? Have I done anything wrong, Uncle Baboon?'

'No, no, not yet! But you were just about to have a drink and I had forgotten that children, of your age, are not supposed to drink from this river.'

'Why?'

'If they do, they will die,' Baboon said ominously.

'Why?'

'You ask too many questions. That's just the way it is.'

Nhowa was very surprised, but he knew that children shouldn't ask too many questions, and he was afraid to ask any more. He was very thirsty and, when he saw Baboon drinking from the river, he grew even thirstier. But there was nothing he could do. When Baboon had had enough, he washed his face with cool water from the river. Then they continued on their way. Not only was Nhowa very thirsty but his feet had grown very sore.

'Uncle Baboon,' he pleaded, 'couldn't we sit down and rest a bit? My feet are terribly sore.'

'Sit down and rest! Do you know what you are saying?' exclaimed Baboon.

'Why, is there anything wrong in sitting down for a little rest? I am very tired.'

'Ho ho ho! I can see you are still young. Do you know what they call this jungle?'

'No. What do they call it?'

'This is the notorious "Eat or Be Eaten" jungle. No one would dare to sit down and rest in this jungle.'

Nhowa became very quiet and they continued on their way. They walked and walked and walked and, after a little while, Nhowa felt his head going round and round and round. 'Uncle Baboon,' he said with tears in his eyes.

'What is it?'

'I can't go on. I am very hungry.'

'Look,' Baboon pointed at a tree a short distance in front of them.

'That is a mukute tree,' Nhowa said. 'Are there any hute on it?'

'Let's go and see,' Baboon answered.

When they got to the tree they saw that its branches were at breaking point. They were heavy with black juicy hute berries. Nhowa's mouth watered as he stretched his hand out to pluck a big juicy berry.

'Hold it!' Baboon shouted sternly.

'Why? Did I do anything wrong?' Nhowa said looking at Baboon with big round eyes.

'No, but you were about to. I forgot to tell you that in this jungle, whenever you see a fruit tree, children always shout, "Mine are

Nhawo could only watch as Baboon washed his face with cool water.

the unripe berries," and the elders shout, "The big juicy ripe ones are for me!"'

'Why is that?' Nhowa asked, a big tear rolling down his left cheek. He was very very hungry. He had never ever been so hungry before.

'Are you asking me, Why?' Baboon glared at him as if he had done something he should never have done. 'Do you want to die? Didn't I tell you the name of this jungle?'

'Eat or Be Eaten,' Nhowa said in a low fearful voice.

'Yes. Remember that name and, don't say it too often, or we will never leave the jungle alive.' Baboon whispered, as if he too, were afraid of something he couldn't see. Then he began to gorge himself on the big ripe hute berries. Nhowa sadly picked at a few of the green unripe ones but they were very hard and bitter. He forced himself to eat them as he was so hungry and thirsty, but he soon gave up. Tears rolled down his cheeks as he watched the thick brown berry juice trickling down Baboon's chin. He wished he had never set out on the journey, but his father had told him he should. He couldn't have disobeyed his father. But, he asked himself, did his father know about the dangers of the jungle? He had never mentioned them.

Nhowa promised himself that he would ask his father when he

got back home. That was, he thought sadly, if he didn't die on the way, because he was now very afraid and very very hungry and his feet were very sore.

When Baboon had eaten his fill of berries, they continued on their way. Nhowa felt relieved that at least they were now walking slowly. Baboon had eaten so many berries, that his belly almost dragged on the ground and he could no longer walk so fast.

They passed many other fruit trees. Baboon always fed himself on the juicy ripe fruits while Nhowa chewed a few of the unripe ones. He felt he had better keep quiet. There were many things he wanted to ask Baboon, but he dared not open his mouth. So they went on and on and on.

A little before sunset, they emerged out of the jungle and on to a grass plain with a scattering of a few green shrubs. They had walked just a little way when Baboon said, 'Look,' pointing to a small bush that grew a little way from their path.

'What is it?' Nhowa asked, hoping that it was something he could eat; something that only children were allowed to eat.

'Do you see that shrub?'

'Yes.'

'Good. Now, its leaves are very good for burns and blisters. So, should you ever hear me cry, "I am burning! I am burning!" you must run quickly to this shrub and bring me some of its leaves. Don't forget.'

'No, I won't forget.'

A little later, just as the sun was setting, they reached the home of Baboon's relatives who were happy to see them. They gave Baboon and Nhowa some water to drink and, while they rested, they prepared them some sadza and relish. When Nhowa saw the steaming sadza and the big pot of stew, his mouth watered. He said to himself, 'It is a good thing that I haven't eaten anything all day. Now I can fill my tummy up without feeling that I have eaten too much.' He thought that his Uncle Baboon wouldn't be able to eat very much as his belly was still swollen from all the wild berries he had eaten before.

10

They washed their hands. As he was the eldest, Baboon was the first to eat. Then, just as Nhowa was about to put a morsel of sadza into his mouth, Baboon jumped up and, spitting out what he had taken, cried out as if he were in pain, 'I am burning! I am burning!' And, he did sound as if he was really burning. Without another thought, Nhowa stood up and rushed out. He made for the place where they had seen the little shrub which Baboon had told him was called mundatsva.

When Nhowa returned with some mundatsva leaves, he found that Baboon had finished all the food. Only a few crumbs of sadza remained. Nhowa ate these and chewed at a few bones which Baboon had thrown on the floor after eating all the meat off them. He cried and cried but there was nothing he could do, because Baboon was talking with his relatives and Nhowa felt that it would be rude to disturb his elders in case they were discussing important matters.

All that night Nhowa couldn't sleep. He dreamt of mountains of steaming sadza and huge pots of meat.

Baboon called him very early the following morning to begin their journey home. Nhowa thought he should say that he needed something to eat, but soon realized that Baboon wouldn't listen to him. Also, he had begun to understand that Uncle Baboon wasn't as good as he had first thought him to be.

On their way back, Nhowa once more ate the unripe fruits, while Baboon greedily ate the ripe ones.

Hare was pleased to see them home safe and sound, although he didn't like the look of Nhowa who seemed pale and tired.

'Are you ill?' Hare asked his son.

'It is a long journey,' Baboon answered quickly before Nhowa could say anything. 'Your son is still too young for such a journey.'

Baboon then fixed Nhowa with a look that said, 'If you say anything about our journey to your father, I'll skin you alive!' After some little grown-up talk about the journey, Baboon left for his house.

After he had gone, Nhowa told his father about everything that had happened on the journey and the Eat or Be Eaten jungle.

'There is no jungle with such a name,' said Hare, when Nhowa had finished his story.

'But why did Uncle Baboon tell me all those lies?'

'I don't know. But you had better quickly run along to your mother and get something to eat. Forget about Uncle Baboon. I am going to talk to him about it.'

But Hare didn't talk to Baboon. He thought he would wait for a good moment. He didn't have to wait long. Six months later Baboon returned to ask Hare if Nhowa could accompany him again on the journey to see his relatives. Baboon didn't think that the young hare could have talked to his father about the previous journey, because Hare had said nothing to him.

When he heard Baboon's request, Hare said, 'I am very sorry, my friend. I have just sent Nhowa to see his grandmother who is very ill. But if you don't mind, I would like to make the journey with you, as I have a little business to settle with your relatives, the Monkeys.'

Baboon didn't want to travel with Hare but he was afraid to journey alone through the jungle. So he said, 'Oh, that's fine. But why do you want to see the Monkeys? What have they done this time? You know, I don't trust those little impostors.'

'It is a matter of honour and trust. You will hear of it when I am through with them,' responded Hare.

'I hope you fix them good and properly. They have been causing my people a lot of trouble lately,' Baboon said firmly.

'So, we start very early tomorrow, do we?' Hare asked.

'Yes, and, don't worry about the food we shall need on the way. I will provide it.'

'Very well. I was a little worried about how I was going to carry two pouches. You see, I have always to carry my medicine with me, as I have an illness that must be treated three times a day.'

Baboon finished all the food, leaving only a few bones.

'Oh, how terrible. What happens if you forget the medicine?' asked Baboon.

'That will be the end of me,' said Hare with conviction.

'Then don't forget the medicine whatever you do,' said Baboon who thought he had better feign kindness.

Very early the following morning, Hare and Baboon began their journey. They travelled on and on and on and as they travelled, Hare occasionally sipped from his bag. Baboon became very thirsty and hungry. He had thought that they would reach the Makudo River, before the sun began to get really hot, but Hare had suggested they go another way, which he said was much shorter. As Baboon watched Hare sipping from his bag, he began to feel hungrier and hungrier and thirstier and thirstier. Moreover, each time Hare took a sip of medicine, he seemed to regain his strength. So, when Baboon saw the medicine trickling from the corners of Hare's mouth, he began to suspect that it wasn't really medicine. He thought of asking Hare about it, but he kept quiet.

The sun was now right above their heads and they still hadn't reached the river. Hare was setting a killing pace and Baboon began to feel pains in his legs. Hare was now doing all the talking: all Baboon could do, was nod his head or grunt some meaningless noise. Then, just after midday, Baboon began to lag behind.

'What's wrong, my friend?' Hare asked.

'Oh, nothing. Just a little pain in a toe that I hit against a tree stump in my fields yesterday.'

And they went on. Then Hare began to run. When he was a little way ahead, he would sit down to rest and take some of his medicine. When Baboon reached him, Hare would stand up and start to run again. Finally, Baboon couldn't bear it.

'I think we are lost,' he said after he had caught up with Hare for the fifth time.

'No, I don't think so,' Hare replied.

'We should have crossed the Makudo River by now,' Baboon argued.

'Not along this path. If we had taken your route, yes. But now the river is bending away from us. We are almost parallel to it. It won't be long before it takes another turn towards our path. What's wrong? Do you want to turn back?' Hare asked this question in a way that made Baboon feel ashamed of himself. He thought Hare considered him a coward.

'Oh, no, no, no! It just crossed my mind that we should have come to the river a long time ago.'

Hare looked at him long and carefully and said, 'Or are you hungry?' Baboon thought of saying no, but he thought he might die if he didn't tell the truth. 'Well, just a little. I was thinking that when we reached the river, we could have a little water to drink. After that, it won't be long before we get to the jungle with all its fruit trees.'

Hare looked at him again and then, as if he really felt sorry for him, said, 'Look, let me give you some of this medicine. It is a kind of food in itself.'

'Do you think it will be all right for me to have some?' Baboon asked eagerly.

'Perfectly all right except . . .'

'Except what?' Baboon was a little disappointed. He suspected that Hare wasn't going to give him the medicine after all.

'Except that you must not eat or drink anything else all day today.' There was a pause while Baboon thought about the consequence . . . If Hare is taking the medicine, and he is still so strong, there won't be any need for me to eat anything for rest of the day, will there . . .

'I will have the medicine,' Baboon said, stretching out his hand.

'Well, don't say I haven't warned you,' Hare replied, offering his bag to Baboon.

Baboon put the bag to his mouth. He took a little of the medicine, rolled it round his tongue, and then greedily put his mouth round the mouth of the bag. He took five big gulps. He looked as if he wasn't going to stop, when Hare shouted, 'Hey! Enough! That's my medicine, remember!'

Baboon greedily put his mouth round the mouth of the bag.

Baboon removed the bag from his mouth reluctantly. 'It tastes like honey,' he said, wiping his lips.

'It is mixed with honey,' Hare said. 'Now, can we continue?'

And they went on their way. A little later they came to Makudo River.

'Ah, water at last!' Hare said as he knelt down to take a drink from the river. But before he could do so, Baboon, who was now very thirsty from both the honey and the journey in the burning sun, quickly raised his hand and said, 'Hold it, friend!'

'Why, what's wrong?' Hare pretended to be surprised.

'Nothing, but I forgot to tell you that this is Baboon country. Only people of the Baboon totem may drink from this river.'

'What happens if you are not of the Baboon totem and you have a drink?'

'You will die,' Baboon said emphatically, looking at Hare with an eye that dared him to break this ancient custom.

Hare looked at the flowing water longingly then, sighing, he stood up, quietly unslinging his bag from his shoulder as he did so.

'I am sorry, friend. I should have told you about this before, but custom is custom,' Baboon said with a thin smile, as he knelt down for a drink.

'Hey, what are you doing?' Hare shouted. Baboon quickly turned to face Hare and said, 'Why, what's wrong?'

'You forget the medicine? What did I say about the medicine?'

16

Baboon slowly pulled himself up to his feet, saying, 'I thought you meant food, that I shouldn't eat any food after taking the medicine.'

'I said anything! If you had listened to me carefully you would have heard me correctly. If you drink that water, as sure as my father's name is Magen'a, your people will bury you tonight. You won't even live to cross this river.' Hare's voice held such authority that Baboon actually saw himself being lowered into the grave. For a moment his thirst left him. 'Well, I'm sorry,' he said, backing away from the water, as if it were some beast that was about to spring at him.

'Well, it's me who should really be sorry,' Hare said sadly, 'I gave you the medicine. I shouldn't have done that.'

'Well, let's continue,' Baboon said. He didn't want to stay longer at the place where he had nearly met his death.

They crossed the river with Baboon walking ahead. He didn't look back. And so he didn't see that Hare had left his medicine bag behind. Then, when they had gone beyond a little low hill on the opposite side of the river, Hare suddenly exclaimed, 'Oh dear, I've forgotten my bag by the river!'

'You go and get it and I'll wait for you here,' Baboon said.

So Hare went back to the river bank and, while he was there, he had a long cool drink of water. Then he collected his bag and joined Baboon who was waiting for him.

'Got it?' Baboon asked as Hare approached. Hare showed him the bag.

'Lucky none of the Monkey totem passed that way. Your people would be burying you tonight,' muttered Baboon who was feeling surly.

'Quite true, quite true,' Hare replied and then they both laughed to think how close to death they had been. At least, that is what Baboon thought.

On they went. They walked and walked and walked and still they hadn't reached the wild fruit jungle. Baboon was now terribly thirsty and the idea of the juicy hute berries danced in his mind.

17

'We should be in the wild fruit jungle by now,' he said when he couldn't keep the thought to himself any longer.

'Didn't I tell you that we crossed the river at a place further west?'

'So you did, so you did,' Baboon said. And then, clearing his throat, he said, 'If it isn't too much bother, could I have a little more of your medicine?'

Hare stopped suddenly as if he had heard some unmentionable horror. He stared long and unblinkingly at Baboon. Baboon felt uncomfortable confronted with such a stare. He stammered, 'Wh- - wh - did I say something I shouldn't have said?'

Hare cut him short, 'Of course you did, you fool!' and he kept staring at Baboon, as if he had never seen such an idiot in all his life. Baboon looked down at his feet and Hare shook his head saying, 'I am sorry, my friend. It's really all my fault. But really, I would have thought that at your age you would know what an overdose of medicine could mean. Have you never heard of such a thing?'

'Yes, of course,' Baboon said quickly, 'but I had forgotten all about it.'

'Well, next time you must not forget about such things, if you value your life. This is medicine, not food!'

After this exchange of words they walked on in silence. Baboon was beginning to resent Hare. His throat was parched from the heat of the sun and the honey that he had drunk. It was taking them such a long time to get to the wild fruit jungle and all because Hare had said he knew of a shorter route. Baboon began to feel he hated Hare. So when Hare said something, Baboon would not answer. Hare saw that Baboon was sulking and he began to trot. It was all that Baboon could do to keep up with Hare's nimble pace. There was fire in his chest and he felt as if rocks were tied to his feet. As he lagged behind, he thought of all the nasty things that he would do to Hare, once he got the chance. When Hare realized that Baboon was simmering with anger, he began to sing and dance and Baboon got crosser still.

And then they were in the wild fruit jungle. Hare waited for Baboon to catch up with him before they entered the forest. 'We shall soon be at your people's home,' Hare said pleasantly.

'Yes, indeed,' replied Baboon vengefully, as if he was going to cook Hare for supper.

'Look!' said Hare when they had gone a little way into the jungle, and pointed at a mukute tree that was black with the ripe juicy berries. Without another word, the two friends made for the tree.

Hare plucked a berry and was about to throw it into his mouth, when Baboon shouted, 'Hold it, friend!' Hare looked at Baboon, the berry still in his hand. He said, 'Did I do anything wrong?'

'You forgot. I told you this was Baboon territory?'

'I thought you meant that I could not drink the water.'

'I thought you would realize that I meant the fruit as well. After all, both go into your stomach, don't they?'

'Oh well, let's go then,' replied Hare, but Baboon was already plucking a berry from the tree. Quickly, Hare grabbed Baboon's hand before he could put the berry in his mouth. He shouted, as if to a child playing with fire, 'The medicine! Won't you ever understand? You took the medicine! Do you want your people to kill me? You know that they would blame me for giving you some of my medicine?'

For a moment the two friends stared at each other. There was a murderous fire in Baboon's eyes, but Hare's eyes were equally piercing. It was as if he was saying, 'You eat this berry, and you will die right now!'

Finally, Baboon let go of the berry, and Hare released Baboon's arm.

'Well, let's go on!' Baboon shouted angrily as he led the way forward. He was so cross that again, he didn't see that Hare had unslung his medicine bag and thrown it on the ground.

Then, when they had gone round a little bend in the path, Hare said, 'Oh dear, Oh dear, I have forgotten my bag again.'

'Oh no, not again!' Baboon exclaimed. 'Next time you forget

Hare plucked two handfuls of berries.

your bag, I won't wait for you.' But he waited for Hare as he also needed a rest from their long, hungry, thirsty walk.

At the mukute tree, Hare plucked two handfuls of berries and threw them into his mouth. After having drunk a lot of honey from his medicine bag, he wasn't really very hungry, but he knew the berries would quench his thirst. Then he collected his bag and joined Baboon who was waiting for him.

'Well, on we go,' Hare said cheerfully when he reached Baboon. Baboon hated Hare's cheerfulness. He felt his hatred growing, right from the bottom of his heart. He searched his mind for something to say that would really hurt Hare, but all he managed was, 'One of these days the Monkey people are going to steal your bag and that will be the end of you.'

'It looks as if I am lucky, doesn't it?' Hare said, winking at his fuming friend. Baboon could have killed Hare, right there and then, but Hare was already ahead of him. So Baboon followed behind, huffing and puffing and fuming and scheming about what he was going to do to Hare.

On they went through the forest of fruit trees and from each tree Hare plucked a fruit and tossed it into his mouth. Baboon, in his anger, didn't notice what Hare was doing. On and on they went, until they came to the little mundatsva shrub. Then Baboon said, 'Look! This little shrub is good for burns. If you ever hear me calling out, "I am burning, I am burning," you must fetch me its leaves.'

'Very well,' answered Hare. Then he moved closer to the shrub saying, 'Let me take a careful look at it, as it is now growing dark.' Then, while Baboon wasn't looking, Hare plucked a few of the leaves and put them into the little pouch that he always wore round his waist.

At last they reached the home of Baboon's people. The Baboons gave them a very warm welcome and water to wash the dust of their long journey away. Then the Baboon girls prepared their visitors a hot meal of sadza and chicken.

When Baboon and Hare had bathed and the meal was ready, the girls brought in the steaming hot food. Baboon dipped his finger into the sadza and then jumped up crying, 'I am burning! Quick, I am burning!' Immediately Hare produced the leaves of the mundatsva shrub from his pouch and gave them to Baboon.

Baboon glared at Hare but took the leaves all the same, squeezed them and applied the juice to his finger. While he did this, Hare began to eat. Baboon wanted to remind Hare that this was Baboon territory, but he knew that his own people would expose his lie. Hare was a special guest and they wouldn't want him to go hungry. He looked at Hare, eating away as if nothing had happened, and swore that he wouldn't eat from the same pot. But when he saw Hare chewing a chicken bone with relish, Baboon threw his pride to the winds and stretched out his hand to grab a chicken leg.

Immediately Hare grabbed Baboon's hand. Baboon looked at

him furiously and Hare pointed at his medicine bag. The other Baboons saw this and asked what was happening. Hare coughed twice, 'Ahem, Ahem.' Then he said, 'Well, it's a bit hard to explain. But I'll try. You see, we took a rather longer route than usual, but my friend hadn't made any provisions for the journey and so it wasn't long before he was hungry. Now, as you see, I carry this bag with me. It is my medicine bag. I suffer from an illness which means that I must take a little medicine every now and again. Since the medicine is mixed with honey, I thought that if I gave a little to Baboon, as he really was very hungry, it wouldn't do him any harm. But I had forgotten to tell him that, after taking the medicine, he was not supposed to eat. I just couldn't see him die of hunger, when I knew I could heip.' Hare coughed once and continued eating.

'But what about you?' an elderly Baboon asked, seeing that Hare was eating and yet he had taken medicine.

Hare coughed again and said, 'That's why I said it could be difficult to explain. After one has taken the medicine for as long as I have, one can eat anything. However, when I first took the medicine, the n'anga only gave me one throatful but I still had to spend the following three days tied up hand and foot. Otherwise I might have injured myself or someone around me. You see, about half a day after taking the first drop of medicine, one suffers from hallucinations which can make one very violent . . .'

At that moment, Baboon, who had been staring at Hare in disbelief, jumped up shouting, 'He is a liar! He is lying! Kill him! Kill him!' Baboon lunged at Hare's throat, but Hare jumped out of his way and Baboon hit his head hard against the opposite wall of the hut and became unconscious for a few seconds.

'You see?' continued Hare looking at Baboon's relatives, 'I have been expecting this all day. Instead of the normal one throatful of medicine, Baboon took five. I only realized this afterwards. But Baboon must be quite strong. No one else could have survived

As Baboon grabbed a chicken leg, Hare grabbed his hand.

22

such a dose. I am really very sorry, but he should be all right, that is if he does not eat or drink for three days.

'Also, if I were you, I would tie him up. There is no telling what damage he could do if you let him loose. I am sorry but he is my friend and I couldn't let him die of hunger in the jungle.' Hare began to sob.

'No, no, no, Hare. It isn't your fault at all . . .' the elderly Baboon had begun . . . when Baboon, who had woken up although he was feeling groggy, cut him short with, 'I tell you, he is lying! He stopped me from drinking water, he stopped me from . . .'

'Better tie him up, boys,' the elderly Baboon ordered the young Baboon men who were in the guest house. So they hurriedly picked up Baboon who was still trying to tell his side of the story and carried him outside where they tied him up and locked him into another smaller hut.

'But isn't there any medicine to cure such madness?' a young girl Baboon asked.

'No.' said Hare firmly. 'If you eat or drink anything, anything at all, after taking my medicine for the first time, then your people will surely bury you that very day.' Hare was emphatic.

'What I don't understand,' pondered the elderly Baboon, 'is why he didn't carry any food, when he knew the journey would be a long one?'

Hare shrugged his shoulders and said, 'I asked him the same thing. Maybe you should ask him yourself?'

'I will,' the old Baboon said.

'But,' Hare raised a finger in warning, 'after three whole days. Otherwise you won't get a coherent word out of him. Worse still, his condition may not improve.'

'Of course we will do as you say,' the wise old Baboon replied. Then he shouted to the young Baboon girls, 'Girls, where are your manners? Don't you see that our guest's meal is getting cold? Come on, get him some more hot food!'

'No, no, grandfather. I am enjoying what . . .'

'No, Hare,' replied the wise old Baboon, 'have some hot fresh food. If we cannot thank you enough for the help you have given to our foolish relative, we can at least feed you well. One good turn deserves another.'

'You couldn't have uttered a truer word,' Hare replied as he fell on the fresh sadza with renewed appetite.

After Hare had eaten, beer was brought, and they sat talking and drinking and laughing until the small hours of the morning. All through the night they could hear Baboon shouting and howling in the little hut in which he had been locked up.

A little before sunrise, Hare began his journey home. In addition to his medicine bag, he carried a large roast chicken prepared for him by the beautiful young Baboon girls and a calabash of corn beer which the wisest old Baboon had given him saying, 'This is to clear the dust from your throat on your long journey back home.'

After thanking them warmly for all their hospitality, Hare's last words words were, 'Remember! Three days.'

The Prince and the Leper

One day, a long time ago, the people of Gasva Village woke up and saw a very beautiful house on top of Gasva hill, the home of their ancestral spirits. The house had not been there the day before. It had just grown out of the night like a strange mushroom. From the village they could see that the walls of the house were the colour of the granite boulders of the hill. Its roof glittered in the sun so that one could not look directly at it on a cloudless day. The chief and the elders of the village were puzzled. Nothing of the sort had ever happened before. Was this the end of the world? Or was it a special sign from their ancestors who were buried in the caves of the hill? They consulted the most powerful n'angas of the village. The n'angas were just as baffled as they were. Finally, the elders thought that they would just wait and see. 'If it is a message about something that we should do, then the message will come,' they said to themselves. In the meantime, they told their people not to go up the hill.

Despite this advice, some daring hunter soon brought word that the owner of the house was a woman. He had seen her working in a corn field close to the house, but he hadn't been able to talk to her. A woman on the hill? Who had built the house for her? Who could she be? Where had she come from? What powers had she that she could just build her house on the very hill on which the elders and founders of the village were resting? She must be a witch. She must be one of the long-gone Aunts of the Tribe. What did she want? The elders and people of the village kept asking themselves these questions and then giving themselves answers – but they didn't know if they were right or wrong.

Then one day, an old woman who had gone to gather fruits on the hill brought them more news. As she was almost completely

The old woman felt herself being taken by the hand.

27

blind and had no one to help her gather firewood or fruit, she had gone up the hill and had stumbled on the house without seeing it. She had been surprised to hear someone greeting her. She had recognized the voice as that of a woman. But she couldn't see where it came from. Then she felt herself being taken by the hand and led into a house. There she had been given food to eat and the woman told the old lady a strange story.

The woman on the hill had been the queen of some distant country. For years and years she had been the hosi of the king of this country but she hadn't been able to give him a child. So the king had taken other wives who had given him lots of children. Finally, after a long time, the woman had given birth to a son. He was so fair and beautiful that all those who saw him from afar, thought he was a girl.

But it was her son's beauty that had made the king throw her and her son out of his home. What happened was that the king's lesser wives began to cast magic spells on the son and his mother. They said that the king loved the hosi's son more than their own sons. And, as the boy grew up, mothers and girls in the land began to fight and even kill each other as they competed for the prince's hand in marriage. Finally, the king had been persuaded by his sharp-tongued lesser wives that the hosi was a witch and he had exiled both mother and son. Cast out, they had wandered over many lands until they had found Gasva hill and there they had decided to settle down.

The elders of the village were very, very puzzled by the old woman's story. Finally, they came to the conclusion that she was old and therefore likely to tell ghost stories brewed on the blurring edges of her disappearing memory.

But the idea that there was a woman who lived in the house on the hill had been sown in the people's minds. So it wasn't long before wood-gatherers, hunters and fruit-gatherers had other stories about the woman on the hill. Most of the reports were of her kindness; that she really had a son who was called Sangare; that he lived locked up in a dark upper room in the house and that

Both mother and son were cast out.

he was so beautiful that any woman who set eyes upon him would immediately be struck blind. That was why his mother kept him locked up in the dark room. She was afraid that the young women of the village would fight over him and then the chief of the land would either be forced to kill them both, or to run them out of the country. But how had she come to build the house on the hill, the elders asked. That, no one had dared to ask her.

Now, as it happened, a few years previously a terrible disease in Gasva Village had claimed the lives of all the young men of marrying age. This had left the young girls without any prospects of getting married and their daily dreams were of handsome young men who would come to marry them. So, when word came down from the mountain that the Queen of the Hill (as they now called her) was looking for a wife for her son, there was panic among the mothers and daughters of Gasva Village. Every mother saw herself as the proud mother-in-law and every young woman saw herself as the envied wife of the handsome prince on the hill.

Pilgrimages were made in secret to the house on the hill by the more daring young women but none of them was brave enough to go very close. There were daily patrols (in the guise of gathering wood or fruit) round the house in the hope that the girls would go up the mountain in groups, each of them hoped that the prince would choose her! But no one saw the young man. Sometimes one of them would see the Queen of the Hill carrying out her daily chores but no one would dare to approach her. Sometimes the queen would look in their direction and the more daring of them would then peep from behind the bush or boulder to look at her (in the hope that whoever was seen would be recommended to her invisible son), but the queen would always turn away as if she hadn't seen them.

The girls made bets, jeered at each other, laughed among themselves, annointed themselves secretly with love potions in the middle of the night, consulted their mothers and aunts, visited old medicine women, prayed to their ancestors and counted the magic love-me-love-me-not leaves of the muzeze tree, but none of them ever saw the young man. There were secret boos and hisses and whisperings as the girls spoke with each other about each other behind each other's back. They paired up and unpaired, grouped, dispersed and re-grouped as each of them tried to choose which of them spoke well of them, or which of them had ill-designs on them. Those who thought they were more beautiful than others chose the company of those they thought were the ugly ones so that their beauty would stand out if ever the prince or the queen happened to see them. Those who thought that they were ugly excelled themselves by working hard in the hope that the queen would think her the most suitable girl for her son.

A small war of words broke out from time to time. Although the girls lived and worked and laughed together for most of the time during that period, each of them was really alone. They knew the prince would choose only one girl for a wife. They wanted to know who that girl was going to be. Some even thought it would be quite good enough to become the second or even third wife of the prince. So they dreamed on torturing themselves and each other. With each passing day, the prince became more and more handsome in their dreams and more and more unattainable in their minds.

Then, somehow, word came down from the mountain that the queen would receive visitors who wanted to see her son. Her son, she said, was unable to come to the village and she couldn't leave him alone, but visitors were welcome, provided that they came in small groups. Each person was allowed only one visit to the house.

It was not long after this that small groups of young women could be seen climbing up the steep path to the house on the hill. The ascent was quite steep and when the girls got to the top most of them were out of breath. They would scramble into the yard and sit down in a group. The queen would then invite them into the house and ask them to sit on the mats that were spread out on the floor. The girls would sit there while the queen prepared them something to eat in the kitchen. When she had finished, she brought sadza and corn beer out to the girls. Because they were thirsty and hungry from the steep climb up the hill, they were always glad to eat the sadza and drink the beer and they always agreed that they had never eaten such delicious food or drunk such delicious beer before. After they had finished, the plates and beer pots did not need washing up as they had been scraped so clean. After she had put away the plates and the pots, the queen went up to her son's room. She stood outside the door and began to sing:
'Sangare, Sangarewo
Come down, come down.'
And the young man sang back:
'Do I hear you calling, Mother?'
'You have some visitors, Sangare.'
'Who are they, Mother?
Who are they?'

'Beautiful girls from the village.'
'Have you given them something to eat, Mother?'
'I have given them sadza.'
'And they have eaten?'
'They have eaten, Sangare.
I have also given them beer.'
'And they drank?'
'They have drunk it all, Sangare.
They have drunk it all.'
'Go back, Mother.
Send them away.
But don't tell them, Mother
Don't tell them
That Sangare will marry
The one who doesn't eat sadza
Sangare will marry
The one who doesn't drink beer.'

After hearing his words Sangare's mother went down the stairs and told the girls to go away. Sangare would not marry any of them. But she wouldn't say why. Sadly, the girls returned to their homes, each of them wondering why Sangare wouldn't marry her.

Every day the girls came, and every day they went back home, their heads lowered. For days and days different girls came to the house on the hill and each time they came Sangare would sing to his mother:
'Go back Mother
Send them away.
But don't tell them
That Sangare will marry
The one who doesn't eat sadza
Sangare will marry
The one who doesn't drink beer.'

They agreed they had never eaten such delicious food.

And every day the girls would wander back to their homes wondering what was wrong with them.

It happened, however, that in the same village there lived another girl called Mapezi. She lived alone in her little dilapidated hut at the edge of the village because her parents had disowned her when she was still very young. The other girls of the village would not play with her. Whenever they went to the river to swim or up to the hills to collect firewood, she would follow them but they would always chase her away. Some would even spit at her although their spit never reached her as none of them dared to get very close to her. Mapezi was a leper.

Every time girls went up the hill, Mapezi would follow them and they would chase her away saying that she would spoil their chances of meeting the prince. Finally, when nearly every girl in the village had been to the hill, Mapezi decided to go too. She simply trailed behind the last group of girls as they went up the hill. This last group was made up of the less confident girls in the

33

village and, although they laughed among themselves, they didn't chase Mapezi away. 'Well, if he wouldn't take the most beautiful girls of the village – who knows – he might decide to marry Mapezi!' they said to themselves and laughed at the idea.

When they got to the house on the hill, the girls sat in the yard until the queen came out to greet them and ask them into the house. The queen didn't notice that there was another girl who was sitting on her own near the ashpit. When Mapezi saw the beauty of the house, she did not dare go any nearer. She wished she had stayed at home. So, when the other girls went into the house, Mapezi remained outside, wishing that the ground would open up and swallow her. She knew she stood no chance of ever being looked at by the prince.

In the house, as usual, the queen brought the girls sadza and beer. When the girls had eaten all the sadza and drunk all the beer, the queen took away the plates and the pots and went to her son's room. She stood outside the door and began to sing:

'Sangare, Sangarewo
Come down, come down.'
'Do I hear you calling, Mother?'
'You have some visitors, Sangare.'
'Who are they, Mother?'
'Beautiful girls from the village, Sangare.'
'What have you given them to eat, Mother?'
'I have given them sadza.'
'And they have eaten?'
'They have eaten, Sangare
I have also given them beer.'
'And they drank?'
'They have drunk it all, Sangare
They have drunk it all.'
'Go back, Mother
Send them away

Mapezi trailed behind the last group of girls.

34

But don't tell them, Mother
Don't tell them
That Sangare will marry
The one who doesn't eat sadza
Sangare will marry
The one who doesn't drink beer.'

And, like the other girls before them, these too went back to their homes with their heads hanging low. As they passed by the ashpit they saw Mapezi sitting there with her head in her hands. Some of the girls began to jeer at her, 'Why don't you go up into the house? He is waiting there for you. He said you are the one that he is waiting for. Go on, go into the house.' Then they began to laugh. Mapezi knew that they were laughing at her. She was so used to this that she didn't pay any attention to what they were saying. She let them go on ahead.

When the girls had disappeared down the hill, Mapezi stood up to follow them. But, at that moment, the queen saw her and called out, 'Do I see someone there?' Mapezi's heart missed a beat with fear. She felt that she had done wrong to come to the house. When the woman called out again, Mapezi felt that it would be rude not to answer her. 'It's only me, Mother.'

'Can I do anything for you?'

'No, no, no, Mother. I was just coming down the mountain and I thought I should take a little rest here.'

'Then you must be hungry and thirsty.'

'Really – I am fine, Mother. A little tired perhaps but I am not hungry at all.'

'Well, come nearer then.'

'I would rather not, Mother. I have to get back home before it grows too dark.'

'There is plenty of sunlight left. You will still reach home before the birds return to their nests for the night. Come.'

Mapezi reluctantly walked up to the house. When the woman

saw that she was about to sit down in the sand just outside the door she said, 'Don't sit there, it's dirty. Come into the house.'

'No, Mother. I am really fine out here,' Mapezi replied timidly.

'But you can't have your food out there,' the queen protested.

'Thank you very much, Mother, but I really don't need any food.'

'You should just have a little beer to wash the dust from your throat.'

'Your kindness is making me feel embarrassed, Mother. I will just sit here quietly for a little while. I don't need anything to eat or drink.'

When the queen saw that she could not persuade Mapezi to come into the house or to eat or drink anything, she sighed and went up to her son's room. She stood outside the door and began to sing:

'Sangare, Sangarewo
Come down, come down.'
'Do I hear you calling, Mother?'
'You have a visitor, Sangare.'
'Who is it, Mother?'
'A beautiful girl from the village, Sangare.'
'What have you given her to eat, Mother?'
'I have given her sadza.'
'And has she eaten?'
'She has refused to eat, Sangare. I also gave her beer.'
'And she drank it all?'
'And she refused to drink it, Sangare.'
'She refused?'

There was a long pause after this, then the young man sang in a voice softer than at any other time:

'Tell her, Mother, tell her
Tell her how I have waited and waited
Waited for her, Mother, waited
For her who won't eat sadza, waited

37

For her who won't touch a drop of beer.
Tell her, Mother, tell her
Tell her I am coming down
Coming down, Mother, tell her
I am coming down.'

When the queen went down to tell Mapezi that her son was coming down to see her, Mapezi didn't know what to do. Panic seized her. She would have run away from the house had the queen not stopped her. 'He said he has been waiting for you,' the young man's mother said gently, trying to sow confidence in Mapezi's heart.

'It's all wrong! There is a mistake somewhere! He definitely hasn't been waiting for me! It's all wrong! Wrong!' Mapezi shouted as if she had suddenly gone out of her mind. She didn't notice that the prince had come down while she was shouting. She only realized that he was standing in front of her when he said, 'No, it isn't wrong at all. It is exactly as it should be.' Mapezi looked at him. He was white. He held his hand up to his face as if he were afraid the light from the sun would burn his eyes. He was slightly bent, as if he was prematurely old. He had lost most of his fingers and toes.

Slowly Mapezi realized that she had found someone who was exactly like her. She felt that whatever she had felt before, whatever she hadn't been able to tell anyone else, she would now be able to tell the young man before her. And, as their eyes met, their smiles mirrored each other's. It was as if they had known one another for a long time and had only been waiting to meet again. And, as they stood there, smiling at each other, the sores and scars on their bodies disappeared.

When word came to the village that Mapezi was going to marry the young man on the hill, none of the girls would believe it. When they went to the wedding and saw Mapezi, they didn't recognize her. They didn't want to believe that it was Mapezi. Still, they thought, the bride wasn't as beautiful as the groom.

Deep inside, each of them wished she had been Mapezi. But what Mapezi knew, that they didn't know, was that not one of them would have taken a second look at the prince, if the queen had allowed them to see him. She knew that no one would have wanted to marry him. But how many of them would believe her if she told them the truth?

Mapezi had married the prince but she felt sorry for the girls of the village who didn't know what they wanted.

As soon as the prince and Mapezi were married, the house on the hill disappeared as mysteriously as it had come. No one ever heard of the prince and the queen again. But, strangely, people of the village began to miss Mapezi.

The Blind Man and the Lion

There was once an old man called Dhigidhi. He lived in a little hut in the middle of a jungle. He lived with a young boy. They had both been left behind when the people of their village ran away from some marauding lions that had begun to attack and kill them.

'Take me with you,' the old man cried when the people left the village.

'You will only get us killed,' they said.

'I may be able to help you some day,' the old man pleaded, but they wouldn't listen to him. How could an old blind man help them, the people said to themselves, and they left him there in the village.

After they had gone, the old man wandered about the village alone. He went into the deserted huts collecting food which he put into a sack that he carried on his back. Then, as he entered another hut, he heard the voice of a little child. The child was crying.

'What's wrong, little one?' the old man said when he heard the child.

'My parents have left me alone. They said they couldn't carry me, because they were carrying my brothers and sisters.'

'Stop crying and come with me,' the old man said.

'Thank you,' said the little boy.

'You can thank me when the lions have gone,' the old man said.

'Do you think the lions will eat us?'

'I don't know, but we have to leave the village very fast. Do you see any hills around?'

'I can only see a big forest to the east of us,' the boy said.

'Lead us to the forest then.'

'But isn't that where the lions live?'

The old man collected food from the deserted huts.

41

'The lions won't look for us in the forest because they know that people live in villages.'

And so the old man and the young boy made their way to the jungle. There, the boy helped the old man to build a hut in the topmost branches of a huge musasa tree.

The two of them lived in their hut for many years and the boy grew up to be a big strong young man. During the day they would climb down from their tree house and go into the jungle to search for food and water and, at night, they would return to sleep. They were quite safe from the wild animals up in the tree. The old man taught the young man some of the things he knew about his people's ways and how to hunt for honey and little animals like hares and reed buck.

One day, the old man said to the young man, 'I am getting very old.'

The young man laughed and said, 'You are still quite fit and strong.'

'What will you do when I die?'

'Don't talk like that,' the young man pleaded with the old man.

'Even if I don't talk about it, nothing is going to change the fact that I shall die quite soon.'

'I wish there was a way to keep death away,' the boy said with tears in his eyes.

'There is no way. I shall die one day and you will be all alone.'

'Then, if you die, I will also die.'

'But you don't have to die before your time.'

'Then what do you think I should do?'

The old man thought for some time and said, 'I think we should find you a wife.'

'We are all alone in this jungle. Where do you think we could find a wife for me?'

'We will search for her.'

'Where?'

They built a hut in the topmost branches.

'Just do as I say and don't talk so much,' the old man said sternly.

And so, on the following day, the two destroyed their hut and went into the jungle to begin their search for a wife. They travelled for many days through the jungle. They slept up trees during the night. They trapped for hares, mice and birds which provided food on their journey.

One day the old man stepped on something that felt like a stone and yet he knew it wasn't a stone.

'What is it I have stepped on?' he asked the young man.

'A tortoise,' the young man replied.

'Pick it up,' the old man said.

On another occasion, the old man stepped on something that felt like a long stick yet he knew it wasn't a stick.

'What is it that I have stepped on?' he asked the boy.

'It is a gun,' the young man said.

'Pick it up,' the old man said.

The young man picked up the gun and they went on. After several days in the jungle they came to an open plain.

'Look!' the young man shouted excitedly.

'What is it?' the old man asked.

'It looks like a village,' the young man said.

'Is it a big village?'

'It seems so.'

'Let's approach it.'

As they drew closer to the village, they passed a well where they found two women filling up their waterpots. After exchanging greetings with them, the old man asked for water to drink. When they had drunk, the old man said to the women, 'We are looking for help.'

'What kind of help are you looking for?' one of the women asked.

'Whose village is this we have come to?'

'It is called the Women's Village.'

'The Women's Village? What a strange name. Why is it called that?'

'What is it I have stepped on?' asked the old man.

'Because there are no men in it.'

'There are no men in it? How come?'

'There used to be men here but they were all eaten by the Lion of the Village.'

'Are you saying that this village was founded by a lion?'

'No. There were men here before the lion came. But when the lion came, it ate them all, one after the other.'

'Are you telling me that the lion just ate them and that they didn't fight the beast?'

The women looked at each other as if the old man had asked them a childish question. It seemed to them that he was some kind of simpleton, so they didn't bother to answer him. Instead, one of them asked a question, 'Well, you said you were looking for some help.'

'Yes. We are looking for a wife for my young nephew,' the old man said seriously. The women laughed, as if the old man had made the funniest joke they had heard in years.

'Why do you laugh?' the old man asked.

'We have just told you that there are no men in our village,' one of the women said.

'And so what? He is not going to marry a man.'

'You don't seem to understand. The lion will not allow any man to live in the village. Very many strong brave men were eaten by this lion.'

'Maybe that is why they were killed. They were too strong and too brave. Is it possible for us to see this lion?' the old man said seriously, which brought more laughter from the women.

'Are you joking?' one of the women asked.

'Do I look like one who would joke?' the old man said.

'We can see that you have a gun and that you are old and blind. The men who were killed by this lion also had guns and not one of them was old or blind,' one of the woman said impatiently. She seemed to think that the old man was making a joke of their menfolk who had been killed by the lion.

'I know, I know,' the old man persisted patiently.

'Well, if you know, then you will please not waste our time with your foolishness.'

'At least give us a place to sleep for the night,' the old man pleaded with them.

'So that when the lion kills you, your spirit will haunt us, because we let him kill you? No, thank you. Go your way! And we would advise you to leave our village quickly because the lion will soon return from its hunting and, if it smells your presence . . .'

'Don't you have a headman in the village? Someone we could talk to?'

'I am the headperson of the village and I am telling you to leave before it's too late.'

'Then you have nothing to fear. If anything happens to us, then I shall have brought it on us myself. Just give us a place to spend the night and . . . maybe . . . you won't regret it.'

'Why do you laugh?' the old man asked the women.

The lion jumped back at the sight of the 'tick'.

Once more the women laughed but to humour the old man and his young nephew, they led them into the village.

In the village, the women came to see the foolish old blind man and his nephew. They gathered around and asked them all sorts of questions. The old man knew that the women were laughing at him but he didn't mind. More than once the young man asked him, 'Don't you think we should take the women's advice and go away before the lion comes?'

'Don't you want a wife?' the old man asked the young man.

'But what use will she be to me when I am dead?'

'And who said you are going to die?'

'It's clear from the stories of these women that the lion will make short work of us.'

'That is the women's story . . . what is your story?'

'I don't . . . think we will see the sun tomorrow.'

48

'I haven't seen the sun for over half my life but am I dead?'

The young man couldn't say anything to this.

Then the women brought lots of food for them. 'At least you won't die hungry!' the women joked and the old man laughed with them.

After supper, the women showed Dhigidhi and the young man the hut in which they were going to spend the night.

'Lock the door!' one of the women said and the others laughed.

'Don't you think we should take this chance and run?' the young man whispered to the old man when they were alone in their hut.

'Have you got the tortoise?' the old man asked him instead.

'Yes.'

'And the gun?'

'Yes.'

'Good. Let's go to sleep.' And, as soon as he had said this, the old man began to snore. The young man could not sleep. Whenever sleep drew near him, he thought he saw a huge shaggy lion standing before him and roaring. Then, towards dawn, he did really hear the heavy footfall of a lion. It gave one terrible earth-shaking roar and said, 'What fool has the cheek to sleep in my house?'

The young man shook the old man and said, 'It is here, Grandfather! The lion is here!' The old man woke up from his deep sleep and said, 'What is it?'

'The lion! It is here!'

And at that moment the lion asked again, 'What fool has the audacity to sleep in my house?'

'And what fool asks such a foolish question?' the old man answered back.

'I am the man of this place,' the lion said.

'And who do you think is afraid of you?' the old man answered fearlessly.

'Do you want to see my beard?' the lion said as it plucked out some long thick hairs and pushed them through an opening in the door. The lion's hair was full of ticks. When the old man felt it he gave a contemptuous snort and said, 'If I showed you my beard you would probably run off to hide in your mother's nhehwe. Let me show you one of the ticks that live in my beard.'

The old man then pushed the tortoise through the opening in the door. The lion jumped back a little at the sight of the 'tick' and then he was quiet for some time. So the old man said, 'Are you still there or have you gone back to your mother?'

'Do you want to hear me roar?' the lion responded to the challenge and roared one of its loudest roars. The women of the village trembled with fear although they were safe in their huts. The young man nearly fainted with horror.

'Did I hear a mouse squeak?' the old man called out. 'I didn't hear a thing. Put your mouth closer to the hole in the door and roar harder than you did last time, otherwise I won't hear you.'

The lion then put its mouth to the door and opened it wide to let out a roar. But the old man's gun roared first.

In the morning the women found the lion dead with its legs in the air, lying outside the hut in which the old man and his nephew were sleeping.

And that is how the old man became the Chief of the Women's Village and his nephew got himself a wife who gave birth to the first men who were not afraid of lions.

In the morning the women found the lion.

The Lazy Young Man
and his Dog

There was once a very lazy young man. He lived with his mother who did everything for him, cooked his food and swept his room. She even oiled the one or two old skins that had been left to her son by his father, which he used as clothes. His father, who had loved him greatly, because he was his only son, had also left him his old dog, Dembo.

Dembo was too old to be useful, but he kept the young man company as, all day long, he changed his sitting position against the wall of his mother's hut. Each day of the year, summer and winter, he leant against the wall, basking in the sun while faithful Dembo kept him company. The old dog slept while the young man sat still, but whenever his master moved, Dembo lifted his head and they would rise and move together.

As the old dog had belonged to the young man's father, it was not surprising that his mother claimed that it was Dembo who did all the thinking for her son. The young man didn't see anything wrong in this: after all, Dembo knew everything about his father's life and he didn't.

Time passed quickly by and the young man soon sported a little furry moustache and beard. All the young men of his age had acquired wives and had their own huts, but Dembo's master still lived in his mother's hut and she was not growing any younger. Indeed, the young man's mother now had difficulty with the smallest household task, such as getting the fire started or fetching water from the well. The young man found himself doing these duties, not because he liked or wanted to, but because he was hungry and his mother was often confined to her bed.

Early the next morning the young man left for his mother's village

Whenever the young man did such duties, he showed that he didn't like what he was doing at all. Dembo saw this and, with his eyes, he tried to tell his master to get a wife. But the young man just didn't notice Dembo's signals.

Then the old dog realized that nothing would ever happen if he didn't put his limbs to use. And, after that, the young man bumped into Dembo every time he tried to do something. But the young man still didn't understand the message and he would never have understood what old Dembo was trying to say if his mother hadn't interpreted it for him.

'Old Dembo is telling you to get someone to help you,' she said.

'Someone to help me? Where would I get someone to help me? The only someone I know is you,' her son answered.

'He is saying you should get a wife,' his mother explained patiently.

Suddenly, the beauty and simplicity of the idea struck the young man. Why hadn't he thought of this before? A wife, of course!

But then, just as quickly, another thought came to him. All the wives he knew he only saw at a distance, from the wall of his mother's hut.

'How do I get a wife, Mother?'

'You go into the village, choose a girl you like and tell her that you would like to marry her.'

'It sounds simple.'

'But girls don't generally like lazy, dirty, no-good wall-lizards.'

'Well, I could go to some other village where the girls don't know me?'

The old woman raised her hand, a glint in her eye. Had it happened at last? Had her son started thinking, even working, for his own living? She decided to encourage him. She said, 'If you went to my village, and mentioned me, you wouldn't have any problems at all. All the girls would be dying to marry Kere's son.'

'Who is Kere's son?' the young man asked, wondering whether his mother was talking about the same thing as he was.

'You, of course.' she replied.

The young man suddenly felt very sad. His mother had not long to live and he had only just discovered her name. He realized that his mother must have been somebody in her own village. Would she die before he discovered who she had been? Yes, he thought, he would go to his mother's village and marry the first girl he found. He would bring her home and she would do all the work while he sat listening to his mother's stories.

Then another difficulty occurred to him: decent clothes. He knew his mother wouldn't be able to help him, and he didn't want to borrow anything from the other young men of the village as he hardly knew them. All he needed was a skin to tie round his waist.

He had never been hunting. And he didn't know of anyone who could catch him a reed buck and sell him the skin. As the young man thought of hunting, old Dembo rubbed himself against his legs. He looked down at the dog, his hopes flickered for a moment and then faded away. Old Dembo was toothless and he could only hunt in his dreams.

Suddenly, a thought entered the young man's mind. Even old Dembo seemed to know this. Tomorrow, the young man felt with an unaccustomed surge of energy, tomorrow he would bring a wife home. He would kill old Dembo and take his coat . . .

Very early the next morning the young man left for his mother's village. He hadn't a worry in his mind. His mother's directions had been very clear. It would take him a good half-day's travel. He had scrubbed himself thoroughly with ruredzo and a spongy stone. He had rubbed wild apple juice into his hair, so that now it was twisting itself into thick manly braids. His face, body and limbs were gleaming with peanut butter oil. And he was sporting a grey and black loin skin which, although still new, was very soft and did not scratch him like his old one. The young man was whistling

He knew that crocodiles would make short work of it.

a tune whose origin he couldn't remember. He couldn't remember his father, so the tune could only have come from old Dembo in their silent hours together. Good old Dembo.

Just at that moment, as he was thinking of old Dembo, he heard a voice singing behind him:

'Give me back my coat
My summer and winter coat.
Couldn't you kill a goat
And not rob me of my coat,
My grey and black spotted coat?'

The young man looked back in surprise. He saw old Dembo trotting after him. He picked up a big stone and hit the dog hard and then he threw him into a ravine and continued on his way.

He felt bad about old Dembo but he had to get a wife. He quickened his pace. Now he could see his mother's village just across the river. As he was about to cross it, he heard the voice again:

'Give me back my coat
My summer and winter coat.
Couldn't you kill a goat
And not rob me of my coat,
My grey and black spotted coat?'

The young man felt very angry with old Dembo. He grabbed him and tied a huge stone round his neck. He knew that crocodiles would make short work of him. But he could not help shedding a tear or two for his old faithful dog.

He crossed the river and after a short walk was in the village. He was told by children he found playing that everyone had gone to the Chief's Court.

'What are they doing at the Chief's Court?'

'Haven't you heard of the Chief's daughter?'

'No. Is she dead?'

The children laughed at him and said, 'No, silly. She was born a mute. She cannot talk. So every year the Chief arranges a contest where all the young men compete to try to make her talk. The one who succeeds in doing so will marry the girl.'

The young man thanked the children and proceeded to the Chief's Court. He could hear the noise of cheering crowds, so it wasn't difficult for him to find his way.

The Chief's Court was in a big enclosure of stones. When the young man walked through the main entrance, he found the whole place filled with hundreds of people. They were all laughing and cheering. They were seated in a circle facing the centre where the Chief and his courtiers were sitting on beautifully carved wooden stools. Everyone was dressed in glossy lion and leopard skins and the Chief himself was wearing a very tall headdress of ostrich feathers. They were all looking into the middle of the circle where a finely-dressed young man was doing amazing body-breaking gymnastics. In front of the young man sat a young woman in zebra skins, her ankles, wrists and neck decked in bronze and copper bangles, bracelets and necklaces. In the middle of her shiny forehead was a moon-white shell; her hair was plaited in circular braids knotted at the top of her head. Looking around at the other girls in the crowd, the young man felt that this young woman (whom he took to be the Chief's daughter) was the most beautiful and best-dressed of them all. He sneaked in and sat at the back of the crowd, watching the contest.

57

The people gasped, clapped their hands and cheered at the young man's acrobatics but the Chief's daughter remained aloof. It was as if she was laughing inwardly at the young man. But she could have been a statue for all the feeling she showed.

The young man watched four more young young men twisting and turning and doing somersaults and cartwheels and rolling and walking on their heads and their hands and pulling their faces before the unmoved young woman. Even the Chief and courtiers laughed at some of the young men's antics, but the young woman might have been watching a cockroach struggling in a pot of milk. The young man was fascinated by her cold, unsmiling presence. She did not seem to be part of the gathering of people.

It was during the last of the gymnastic feats that the young man heard the singing. He looked round to see whether anyone else had heard it, so that he could sneak out without attracting attention. But he was too late. Everyone had heard the singing. All eyes turned towards the entrance. The Chief and his courtiers looked the same way. When the Chief's daughter saw everyone staring in the same direction, she slowly turned her head, as if she was afraid her neck would break.

The young man knew that he was in trouble. He lowered his head and shoulders, wishing the ground would open up and swallow him. The singing grew louder and nearer. There was a deathly silence. All eyes were glued to the entrance. Stand up and run? Stand up and go to the Chief and fall on his knees and beg his forgiveness for disturbing the contest? The young man didn't know what to do.

Then old Dembo appeared at the entrance. He stood there tottering on his pink legs, his body skinned, his tongue lolling out. He seemed to be sniffing the air in the courtyard. He raised his head to the sky and howled:

'Give me back my coat
My summer and winter coat

58

Couldn't you kill a goat
And not rob me of my coat,
My grey and black spotted coat?'

At the words, 'my grey and black spotted coat', the young man felt that everyone's eyes focused on him. There was nowhere to hide. There was nothing for him to do but give himself up. So he jumped up. At precisely the same moment, old Dembo sprang up at him.

There was much confusion. People rushed to the other side of the court. The Chief and his courtiers stood up shouting 'Catch him! Catch the intruder!' but no one could hear them. Old Dembo had caught hold of one corner of the young man's loin-skin and was pulling at it. The young man struggled to keep the skin wrapped round him. There was a thick cloud of dust as the two rolled on the ground in front of the Chief and his daughter, who had run for protection to her mother's arms. When the people realized that the dog had only come for one man, they began to cheer and clap their hands, howling with laughter and ululating. Even the Chief and his courtiers were holding their sides because they were laughing so much. Old Dembo wouldn't let go of the coat. The young man felt as if he was fighting for his life. He was panting and sweating, and his eyes looked as if they would jump out of his head.

'Come on, dog! Get your coat! Undress the thief!' the crowd roared. Dust filled the courtyard and Dembo's growls mixed with the young man's panting. The jeering, clapping of hands and stamping of feet made such a noise that when old Dembo finally ripped his coat off the young man, the roar from the crowd was enough to raise the dead.

Then, all of a sudden, there was a silence that would have frightened the dead themselves. The men gasped and the women covered their faces.

The young man stood in the centre of the courtyard as naked as the day he was born. The women were scandalized.

She covered him with her leopard skin.

'Kill the son of a witch!' the Chief was the first to recover.
'Quick! Kill him! Where are you boys? I said kill . . . the . . .'
'No, no, don't kill him, please!'

It was a voice no one, in the whole village, had heard before. It was a voice to wake a dying man. All the people turned towards it and saw the Chief's daughter taking off one of her shoulder skins.

The people gasped in amazement as they saw her rush over to the young man and cover him with her leopard skin.

She held him by the waist and began to laugh. Her laugh seemed to begin at a distance, as if a tiny silver ring had dropped on a rock in the depth of night; then it came nearer, ringing and tinkling like a clear mountain stream tumbling over rocks. The people couldn't believe it. The Chief's wife was the first to gasp, 'She's laughing! My daughter is laughing!' The Chief gave a kind of hiccup and then began to roar with laughter. He laughed so much that the people were dumbfounded. They hadn't heard their Chief give such a roaring laugh since before the birth of his deaf-mute daughter. When they all realized what was happening, the courtyard was filled with another deafening roar of cheering, catcalls, whistling and ululations.

The young man just stood there, with a stupid, frightened grin on his face, while the Chief's daughter knelt before him, holding him tightly round the waist, laughing. The Chief's wife would have rushed to embrace her daughter but the aunts held her back. It was not proper to rub shoulders with a strange young man.

The Chief, recovering from his laughter, raised his hands for silence. Everyone became silent, except the Chief's daughter. She was still laughing. Old Dembo, who now had his coat on, was licking the face of the young woman. The Chief called out softly, 'Miedzo.' It was his daughter's name. The young woman turned her head and spoke softly, 'Father.' At the sound of her voice, another roar went up from the crowd. After the noise had died down, the Chief cleared his voice and said, 'Forgive me, my people. I have never been so happy in all my life. But then, let me first of all greet this stranger who has honoured us today. Come forward, young man. Don't be afraid.'

The young man went forward and stood before the Chief. Miedzo rushed back to the arms of her mother. She could be heard laughing quietly and talking all sorts of nonsense into her mother's ear. Her father dared not ask her to stop talking while he spoke to the young man.

'What is your name, young man?'

'I am Kere's son.'

'Kere's son?'

And the young man told the people where he came from and how he lived with his old mother and what had brought him to the Chief's village. When he was through, the Chief smiled broadly and said, 'You have got yourself a wife.'

'But I am very poor,' the young man protested. The Chief silenced him and said, 'Go back home, collect your mother and then let us all prepare for the wedding together.'

So the young man became the Chief's son-in-law and, surprisingly, one of the Chief's most able courtiers. He lived in the Chief's Court with his wife Miedzo. The young man's mother spent the last few years of her life with her son and new daughter-in-law and it was a happy time for her. The only people who were not happy were the young men who had failed to make the Chief's daughter talk and so could not marry her. But they married other young women who were just as faithful to them as the Chief's daughter was to the young man.

And old Dembo? He was last seen on the day of the wedding as he sat in front of the bride and the groom, gorging himself on the big chunks of meat that the bride kept putting on his plate. He showed his thanks by rising up and sitting on his haunches and licking the bride's face. People said that he behaved like a real mother-in-law. After the wedding, he just disappeared, as is the custom with dogs and cats when they know their time is near and don't want to cause any problems. But old Dembo's song became so popular on the day of the wedding that that is why, even today, we are still singing:

'Give me back my coat
My summer-and-winter coat.
Couldn't you kill a goat
And not rob me of my coat,
My grey and black spotted coat?'

'Let us all prepare for the wedding together.'